9-30-84

A HALLOWEEN
MASK FOR MONSTER

Virginia Mueller

pictures by Lynn Munsinger

Albert Whitman & Company, Niles, Illinois

Library of Congress Cataloging-in-Publication Data

Mueller, Virginia.
   A Halloween mask for Monster.

   Summary: Monster tries on girl, boy, cat, and dog
masks at Halloween but since they are all too scary he
decides to go as himself.
   [I. Halloween—Fiction. 2. Monsters—Fiction]
I. Munsinger, Lynn, ill. II. Title.
PZ7.M879Hal 1986   [E]   86-1569
ISBN 0-8075-3134-0 (lib. bdg.)

Text © 1986 by Virginia Mueller
Illustrations © 1986 By Lynn Munsinger
Published in 1986 by Albert Whitman & Company, Niles, Illinois
Published simultaneously in Canada by General Publishing Limited, Toronto
All rights reserved. Printed in U.S.A.
10   9   8   7   6   5   4   3   2   1

To Donna Pape, my mentor. *V.M.*
To Sarah. *L.M.*

It was Halloween.

Monster tried on a girl mask.

"Too scary," Monster said.

Monster tried on a boy mask.

"Too scary," Monster said.

Monster tried on a dog mask.

"Too scary," Monster said.

Monster tried on a cat mask.

"Too scary," Monster said.

Monster looked in the mirror.

He saw his own face.

"Just right," Monster said.